TABLE OF CONTENTS

Introduction	5
Chapter One Vital Statistics	6
Chapter Two History of the Band	12
Chapter Three Their Music	19
Chapter Four Quotable Quotes	27
Chapter Five Donnie	33
Chapter Six Danny	37
Chapter Seven Jon	41
Chapter Eight Jordan	45
Chapter Nine Joe	49
Chapter Ten Discography & Videography	53
Answers	58

Introduction

They're the hottest act in the music business. Their albums go instant platinum. Their concerts sell out in minutes. They also happen to be five of the cutest guys around! They are, of course: Donnie Walhberg, Danny Wood, Jon Knight, Jordan Knight, and Joe McIntyre—better known to their millions of fans as NEW KIDS ON THE BLOCK. Their meteoric rise to fame has occurred in just a few short years. These five kids from Boston have taken the world by storm. Sure, you have their records, maybe you've even been lucky enough to see them in concert. But how much do you *really* know about your favorite band? Test your New Kids knowledge with the questions and puzzles in this *New Kids on the Block Trivia Quiz Book*. There are questions about their lives, their loves, their music, and much, much more. So get a few of your friends together and see who knows the most about these five fantastic guys. Or just check out your own N.K.F.I.Q. (New Kids Fan Intelligence Quotient). Why, did you know...

CHAPTER ONE

Vital Statistics

1. Who is the youngest New Kid?
2. Who was the first to join the band?
3. Which New Kid has dated Tiffany?
4. Who just loves chocolate milk shakes?
5. Which New Kid loves to go to horror movies on a date?
6. Which New Kid's favorite actor is Robert DeNiro?
7. Whose favorite car is a Black BMW 735?
8. Whose favorite drink is Classic Coke?
9. Whose favorite book is *Old Yeller*?
10. Whose favorite cartoon character is Woody Woodpecker?

NEW KIDS ON THE BLOCK TRIVIA QUIZ BOOK

BY
MICHAEL
TEITELBAUM

Photo Credits:

Title page—Jeff Katz
p. 4—Scott Weiner
p. 7—C.V.D. Vooren/Retna Ltd.
p. 10—Vinnie Zuffante/StarFile
p. 13—Eddie Malluk/Retna Ltd.
p. 16—Ken Berard/Retna Ltd.
p. 20—Larry Busacca/Retna Ltd.
p. 24—Vinnie Zuffante/Star File
p. 28—Larry Busacca/Retna Ltd.
p. 32—Larry Busacca/Retna Ltd.
p. 36—Larry Busacca/Retna Ltd.
p. 40—Vinnie Zuffante/Star File
p. 44—Larry Busacca/Retna Ltd.
p. 48—Larry Busacca/Retna Ltd.
p. 52—Larry Busacca/Retna Ltd.
p. 56—Vinnie Zuffante/Star File

Published by: **Watermill Press**
Mahwah, New Jersey

Copyright © 1990 Kidsbooks, Inc.

ISBN:0-8167-2227-7

All rights reserved including the right of reproduction in whole or in part in any form.

Manufactured in the United States of America

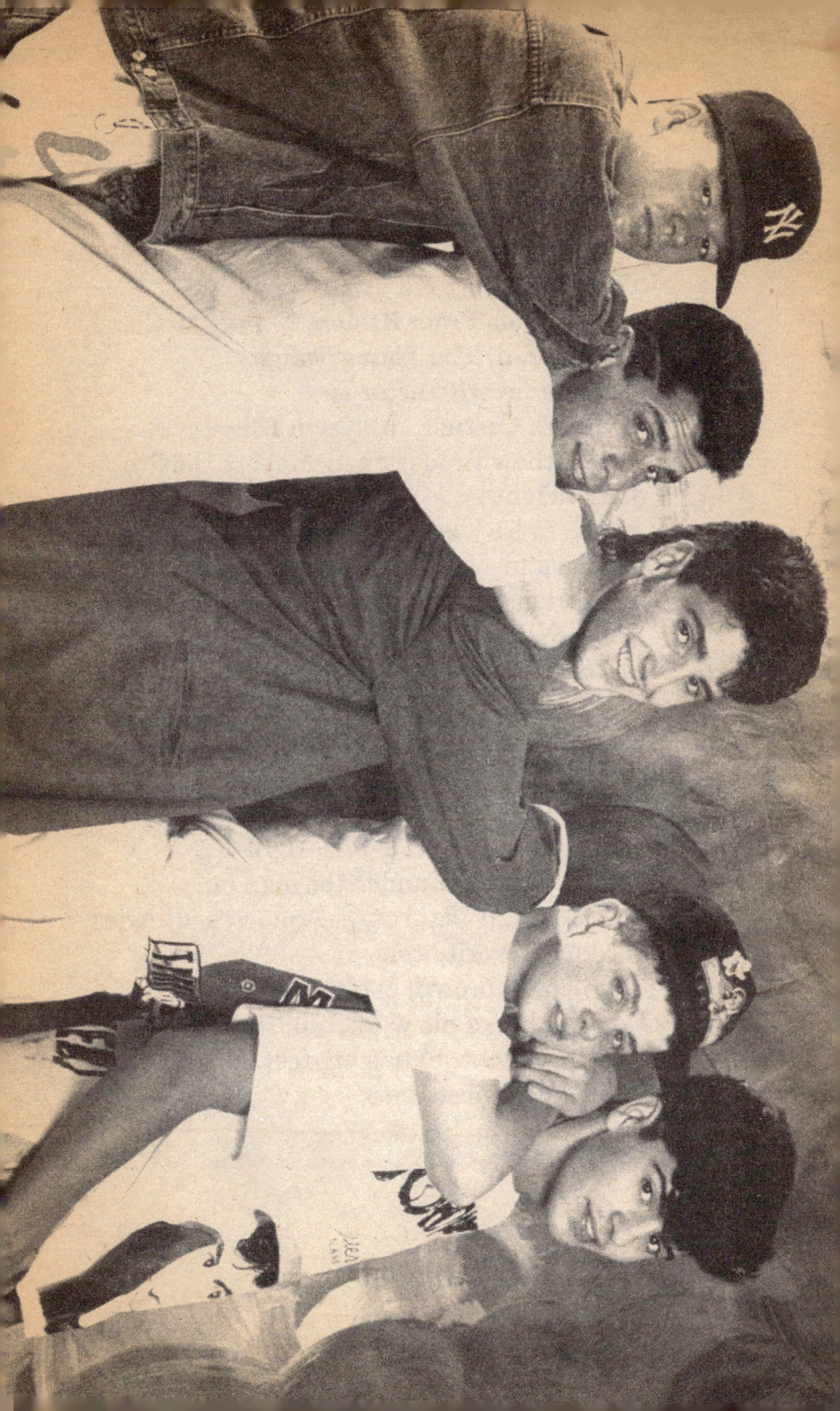

NEW KIDS TRIVIA BOOK

Multiple Choice

11. The band's original name was:
    a) New Kids From Boston, b) Puff McCloud,
    c) Nynuk, d) The Young Toughs
12. Danny's favorite actor is:
    a) Kevin Costner, b) Kevin Kline,
    c) Matthew Broderick, d) Robert DeNiro
13. Joe's height is:
    a) 6', b) 5'6", c) 5'10", d) 5'8"
14. Jordan's favorite vacation spot is:
    a) Florida, b) Jamaica, c) Hawaii, d) California
15. Donnie's favorite TV show is:
    a) *Cheers,* b) *The Cosby Show,*
    c) *Married...With Children,* d) *Sesame Street*
16. The New Kids released their first album in:
    a) 1986, b) 1984, c) 1985, d) 1988
17. Jon's shoe size is:
    a) 8-1/2, b) 9, c) 9-1/2, d) 10-1/2
18. Danny was born under the sign of:
    a) Gemini, b) Taurus, c) Aquarius, d) Aries
19. Jordan's favorite color is:
    a) green, b) brown, c) blue, d) red
20. Donnie thinks his worst quality is that he:
    a) is impatient, b) has big feet, c) is too shy,
    d) has a big nose

NEW KIDS TRIVIA BOOK

True or False

21. Donnie has hazel eyes.
22. Joe's favorite food is Italian.
23. Danny's pet peeve is prejudice.
24. Jordan's type of girl is a loving girl who likes to have fun.
25. Jon's favorite city is Los Angeles.
26. Donnie's favorite thing to do on a date is to go to an amusement park.
27. In the future, Danny would like to be a recording engineer.
28. Joe's favorite sport is baseball.
29. Jon's secret wish is for everyone to be happy.
30. Jordan has five brothers and sisters.

Fill in the Blank

31. _____ and _____ are the two band members who are brothers.
32. _____ and _____ are Jon's two Siamese cats.
33. _____ is the New Kid you'd be most likely to find in the gym.
34. Donnie's musical idol is _____.
35. _____ would some day like to be a journalist.
36. Danny's favorite snack is _____.

NEW KIDS TRIVIA BOOK

37. Jordan has _____ hair and _____ eyes.
38. Danny's two nicknames are _____ and _____.
39. Joe's favorite hobby is _____.
40. Donnie's favorite car is a _____.

Match each New Kid with his birthday

41.	Jon	a)	August 17
42.	Donnie	b)	December 31
43.	Jordan	c)	November 29
44.	Danny	d)	May 17
45.	Joe	e)	May 14

New Kids Scrambles

Unscramble these New Kids song titles:
46. EPASEL TOND OG ILRG
47. ETATR EM GIRTH
48. VOCRE LIRG
49. RAE UYO OWDN?
50. ISHT SONE OFR HET DLIHCNER

CHAPTER TWO

History of the Band

1. Who was the New Kids' producer/songwriter?
2. What other pop band was he responsible for?
3. Who left that band to become a solo success?
4. Who was the New Kids' first manager?
5. In what year was the idea for New Kids born?
6. At what national celebration did the New Kids perform in 1986?
7. What is the first record Danny ever bought?
8. What was Joe's favorite Christmas present?
9. Which record label signed the New Kids?
10. In what year were they signed?

NEW KIDS TRIVIA BOOK

Multiple Choice

11. The number of guys who auditioned for the New Kids was:
    a) about 50, b) over 2,000, c) 10,000, d) over 500
12. The New Kids' second manager was:
    a) Dick Scott, b) Mary Alford, c) Maurice Starr, d) Michael Jackson
13. Donnie's first ambition was to be a:
    a) poet, b) baseball player, c) doctor, d) musician
14. Danny's first ambition was to be a:
    a) lawyer, b) singer, c) architect, d) policeman
15. The total of the New Kids plus their brothers and sisters adds up to:
    a) 30, b) 35, c) 17, d) 41
16. In one year alone, the New Kids sold this many records: a) 5 million, b) 8 million, c) 11 million, d) 14 million
17. Donnie's best buddy growing up was:
    a) Jon, b) Danny, c) Jordan, d) Joe
18. This best buddy was a skillful:
    a) hockey player, b) piano player, c) break dancer, d) song writer
19. The original fifth New Kid was:
    a) Jamie Kelly, b) Bob Hanson, c) Kelly Roberts, d) Dick Starr
20. The "Kid" who replaced him was:
    a) Jordan, b) Joe, c) Danny, d) Jon

NEW KIDS TRIVIA BOOK

True or False

21. Danny was the first one to be selected for the band.
22. The New Kids' first album was a smash hit as soon as it was released.
23. Donnie's brother Mark was once in the New Kids.
24. The Knight family was originally from Canada.
25. Jon's middle name, Rashleigh, is his grandmother's maiden name.
26. Danny has five sisters.
27. Joe never wore braces as a kid.
28. Donnie's family played weekly all-family bingo games.
29. Danny had no singing experience before joining New Kids.
30. Jordan and Jon's parents have taken in over 10 foster children.

Fill in the Blank

31. _____, _____, _____, and _____ all went to the same school in Boston.
32. The name of the school is the _____ _____ _____ School.
33. Donnie's parents names are _____ and _____.

NEW KIDS TRIVIA BOOK

34. Jon and Jordan's parents names are _____ and _____.
35. Joe's parents names are _____ and _____.
36. Danny's parents names are _____ and _____.
37. Donnie has _____ brothers and sisters.
38. Danny has _____ brothers and sisters.
39. Jon and Jordan have _____ brothers and sisters (not counting each other).
40. Joe has _____ brothers and sisters.

Match each New Kid with his nickname

41. Donnie   a) GQ
42. Jon   b) J
43. Danny   c) Joe Bird
44. Joe   d) Dennis Cheese
45. Jordan   e) Puff McCloud

NEW KIDS TRIVIA BOOK

New Kids Secret Code

Use the key below to decipher the secret message. Then use the code to send secret messages (about the New Kids, of course!) to other fans.

The Key

Real letter: A B C D E F G H I J K L M
Code letter: Z Y X W V U T S R Q P O N

Real letter: N O P Q R S T U V W X Y Z
Code letter: M L K J I H G F E D C B A

The Secret Message

WLMG BLF QFHG OLEV

WLMMRV'H QVZMH

CHAPTER THREE

Their Music

1. What is the name of the New Kids' first album?
2. What is the name of their first million selling album?
3. What is the name of their first single?
4. What is the name of their Christmas album?
5. What is the name of the original song they released as a Christmas single?
6. What is Danny's favorite song?
7. What is Donnie's favorite song?
8. What is Jon's favorite type of music?
9. What is Joe's favorite band?
10. What is Jordan's favorite song?

NEW KIDS TRIVIA BOOK

Multiple Choice

11. Donnie plays:
    a) guitar, b) drums, c) piano, d) sax
12. Joe plays:
    a) piano, b) bass, c) lead guitar, d) drums
13. Jordan plays:
    a) trumpet, b) guitar, c) percussion,
    d) keyboards
14. Jon plays: a) sax, b) drums, c) clarinet, d) piano
15. The video for "I'll Be Loving You (Forever)" was filmed in:
    a) Boston, b) Los Angeles, c) Brooklyn, N.Y.
    d) London
16. The video for "You Got It (The Right Stuff)" was filmed in:
    a) New York, b) Louisiana, c) Texas, d) Boston
17. The New Kid who does *not* sing lead is:
    a) Jordan, b) Joe, c) Danny, d) Jon
18. The video for "This One's for the Children" was filmed in:
    a) England, b) Chicago, c) Queens, New York,
    d) Hawaii
19. The New Kid who plays tambourine is:
    a) Joe, b) Donnie, c) Jon, d) Danny
20. The New Kids filmed a commercial for a CD player in:
    a) Los Angeles, b) Japan, c) Ireland, d) Germany

NEW KIDS TRIVIA BOOK

True or False

21. On July 13, 1989 the New Kids were awarded the "USA 1 Man Award" for projecting a drug-free image.
22. The award was presented in their hometown of Boston.
23. The New Kids received two American Music Awards for their album *Hangin' Tough*.
24. The New Kids have released ten music videos.
25. The New Kids all played instruments when they joined the band.
26. The New Kids have foolproof disguises to wear when they go out in public.
27. The New Kids made their TV debut on *Star Search*.
28. The New Kids will star in a movie soon.
29. Jon and Tiffany are secretly married.
30. The New Kids have released three albums.

Fill in the Blank

31. New Kids played in London's Wimbley Stadium in 1989 with _____ and _____.
32. One of the New Kids' biggest thrills was playing at the world famous _____ Theatre in Harlem, New York.

33. The New Kids have been referred to as a 1990s version of _____.
34. Because of their busy schedule, the New Kids are known as "_____ _____ _____ _____ _____ _____ _____ _____."
35. The New Kids have done a lot of work for the _____ _____ _____ Foundation.
36. They participated in that charitable organization's _____ in New York City, to raise money.
37. Massachusetts Governor Michael Dukakis made April 24, 1989 _____ _____ _____ _____ _____ Day in Massachusetts.
38. Governor Dukakis did this to thank the band for _____.
39. On April 25, 1989 the New Kids won the Boston Music award for "Outstanding Music Video" and "Outstanding R&B single" for the song _____.
40. At the same ceremonies Maurice Starr received the _____ award.

NEW KIDS TRIVIA BOOK

Match each New Kids song with the album it appears on

41. *New Kids on the Block* (album)
42. *Hangin' Tough* (album)
43. *Merry, Merry Christmas* (album)

  a) "This One's for the Children"
  b) "Popsicle"
  c) "I Need You"

NEW KIDS TRIVIA BOOK

New Kids Word Search

Find the names of the five band members, their first manager, and their producer in the word block. Look up, down, diagonally, forward, and backward. Some first and last names are together, others have been separated.

The Names

Donnie Wahlberg   Jon Knight
Jordan Knight   Joe McIntyre
Danny Wood   Mary Alford
        Maurice Starr

```
D M C A L N Y O D R U M S K
E O I H E C N N S R O J O N
A N N Y E C I R U A M A R I
E L L N E I N S T T A G R G
I E E N I N S E U S U N I H
L I H A A E L L S M M R U T
E G Y D O O W E S C L C B Y
T A O S O K T A I S I T I A
T O H O N I X N H Y Y R A M
R B A I A A T S D L U E L A
U N G R D Y T R H O B L F U
O H J O R D O I S H D E O R
T M B E O J H C R U H C R I
D O E I J C O N C E R T D G
```

CHAPTER FOUR

Quotable Quotes

WHO SAID:
1. "I love doing the shows. I love being onstage with my friends."
2. "We really do read all the mail that comes in."
3. "I wasn't even a performer when I met Maurice."
4. "I would like to change the way we treat the environment."
5. "I'm confident with myself, but not conceited."
6. "I like meeting fans at concerts and talking to them backstage."
7. "We were very nervous when we first met Tiffany. We wanted to make a good impression because she's really talented."
8. "Horror movies are my favorite kind of movies even if they do scare me sometimes."
9. "A lot of people throw gifts at us on stage. Sometimes it can be scary."
10. "I never dreamed of being a pop star."

NEW KIDS TRIVIA BOOK

Multiple choice

WHO SAID:

a) Danny, **b)** Donnie, **c)** Jon, **d)** Jordan, **e)** Joe

11. "We're not these big, perfect, awesome dudes who can do anything. We're equal to our fans—in fact, we're just like them!"
12. "We can't go into malls and stuff like that. It gets really crazy with the fans."
13. "I admire my mother. She's been a lot of support to me and my career."
14. "I like to go to a dance club or play basketball or soccer."
15. "When our first album didn't take off, we could've just given up. What kept us together was that we're such good friends."
16. "We're from the streets, but we're not hoods or anything."
17. "I'm hoping that everyone could live peacefully together without fear forever."
18. "I'm somewhat of a wise guy. Sometimes I worry, and I like it when everything goes my way."
19. "I'd like to manage a band someday."
20. "Rehearsals can be boring and hard work."

NEW KIDS TRIVIA BOOK

True or False

21. Donnie said: "I'm quitting the group."
22. Joe said: "I have a secret girlfriend."
23. Danny said: "I'd like to be a recording engineer."
24. Jon said: "I bought my mom a brand new Lincoln Continental."
25. Jordan said: "The girls in our videos are our real girlfriends."
26. Donnie said: "We give many of the gifts we receive to charities."
27. Danny said: "Jordan and Donnie got injured in a fight."
28. Joe said: "I would only date a petite girl."
29. Jon said: "Some of the New Kids smoke."
30. Jordan said: "Most of the music for our next album is already recorded."

NEW KIDS TRIVIA BOOK

Fill in the blank

31. Donnie said: "My family had a _____ reputation when I was growing up."
32. Jordan said: "The other guys like to play _____ games on the tour bus."
33. Joe said: "We did a _____ song on our first album called 'New Kids On the Block.'"
34. Danny said: "We love playing _____ _____ on each other."
35. Jon said: "We have a guy who designs our _____ for the stage."
36. Donnie said: "I love my dad's _____."
37. Jordan said: "We recorded the Christmas album in a _____ _____ in two or three days."
38. Joe said: "Stay in _____ and get involved with activities."
39. Danny said: "We have this guy named _____ from Astor Place Haircutting in the Village who does our hair."
40. Jon said "I like the choreography of the old _____ groups."

CHAPTER FIVE

Donnie

1. What was the name of Donnie's first teddy bear?
2. What did Donnie's dad do for a living?
3. Who is Donnie's favorite baseball team?
4. In which Boston neighborhood did Donnie grow up?
5. In what Boston neighborhood did Donnie go to school?

Multiple Choice

6. Donnie started out singing what kind of music?
   a) jazz, b) punk, c) rap, d) folk
7. Donnie formed a band called:
   a) Bad Kids, b) Risk, c) Chill, d) Boston Brats

8. Donnie hung out with a bunch of kids who called themselves: a) The Soda Pop Kids, b) The Lemonade Brigade, c) The Water Boys, d) The Kool Aid Bunch
9. In his quieter moments Donnie loves to: a) draw, b) read, c) build model planes, d) write poetry
10. Donnie likes a girl who is: a) shy, b) strong and independent, c) tall, d) talented

True or False

11. Donnie's favorite kind of date is dinner out and a quiet walk.
12. Donnie loves Ferris wheels.
13. Donnie is a Leo.
14. Donnie is a big fan of the Cookie Monster.
15. Donnie is the youngest New Kid.

Fill in the Blank

16. Donnie's favorite cookies are _____.
17. Donnie loves the colors _____ and _____.
18. Donnie recently recorded a duet with Japan's top female vocalist, _____.
19. Donnie produced a new album by a rap band called _____.
20. This rap band was formerly called _____.

CHAPTER SIX

Danny

1. Danny's middle name, William, was given to name him after which relative?
2. What was Danny's favorite toy as a kid?
3. What did Danny's dad do for a living?
4. What is Danny's favorite place in the world?
5. Which New Kid was Danny's good friend growing up?

Multiple Choice

6. The sport Danny really excelled at was:
   a) football, b) hockey, c) track, d) tennis
7. Who else in Danny's family excelled at this sport?
   a) his father, b) his brother Brett,
   c) his sister Melissa, d) his sister Pamela

8. As a teen-ager Danny was a great:
   a) breakdancer, b) fisherman, c) bicyclist,
   d) tap dancer
9. Danny once belonged to a group called:
   a) The Wild Bunch, b) The Northside Kids,
   c) One World, d) Rock Against Racism
10. In addition to songwriting for the New Kids,
    Danny has also helped them with their:
    a) choreography, b) costumes, c) stage lighting
    d) diets

True or False

11. Danny loves horror movies.
12. Danny hates to sleep late. He's an early riser.
13. Danny will not wear earrings.
14. Danny says he was a "troublemaker" when he was younger.
15. Danny has a quick temper.

NEW KIDS TRIVIA BOOK

Fill in the Blank

16. Danny has _____ hair and _____ eyes.
17. Danny's favorite actress is _____.
18. Danny drives a _____.
19. The holiday Danny loves best is _____.
20. Danny's favorite expression is "_____ _____ _____!"

CHAPTER SEVEN

Jon

1. Where did Jon go on family summer trips?
2. What are Jon's two favorite hobbies?
3. Which older soul group most influenced Jon musically?
4. What is Jon's favorite public television show?
5. What is the license plate number on the car Jon bought for his mom?

Multiple Choice

6. On the New Kids' Christmas album Jon sang lead on:
   a) "Rudolph the Red Nosed Reindeer,"
   b) "Little Drummer Boy,"
   c) "White Christmas," d) "Silent Night"
7. Jon's hair is:
   a) brown, b) black, c) blond, d) red

NEW KIDS TRIVIA BOOK

8. Jon's favorite drink is:
   a) water, b) milk shakes, c) fruit juice, d) iced tea
9. The type of music Jon can't stand is:
   a) rap, b) punk, c) folk, d) heavy metal
10. One of Jon's favorite people on the New Kids team is road manager:
    a) Dick Scott, b) Peter Work, c) Maurice Starr, d) Mary Alford

True or False

11. Jon always likes to dress up.
12. Jon believes that opposites attract.
13. Jon was a good student.
14. His best subject was math.
15. Jon thinks he complains too much.

NEW KIDS TRIVIA BOOK

Fill in the Blank

16. Jon went to a private school called _____ _____.
17. The New Kid who brought Jon into the band was _____.
18. Jon loves to watch _____ cartoons.
19. Jon loves to _____ and _____.
20. Jon has about _____ teddy bears at home in his closet.

CHAPTER EIGHT

Jordan

1. What is Jordan's favorite play?
2. What instrument has Jordan been studying?
3. Who is Jordan's songwriting partner?
4. How does Jordan relax after a concert?
5. Does Jordan ever borrow his brother's clothes?

Multiple Choice

6. What does Jordan put on all his food?
   a) mustard, b) salt, c) mayo, d) ketchup
7. Jordan's room at home is:
   a) very messy, b) always neat,
   c) usually pretty neat, d) too small
8. Jordan collects: a) baseball cards,
   b) stamps, c) hotel keys, d) comic books

NEW KIDS TRIVIA BOOK

9. Jordan's eyes are:
   a) blue, b) brown, c) green, d) hazel
10. Jordan's favorite pastime is:
    a) going to a baseball game, b) going hiking,
    c) jogging, d) going to the beach

True or False

11. Jordan took piano lessons as a kid.
12. Jordan wears braces.
13. Jordan has a steady girlfriend.
14. Jordan had both his ears pierced.
15. Jordan is righthanded.

NEW KIDS TRIVIA BOOK

Fill in the Blanks

16. Jordan graduated from _____ _____ High School.
17. Jordan is scared of _____.
18. Jordan fell asleep in the middle of the movie _____.
19. Jordan is producing an album by New Kids opening act, _____.
20. Jordan's nervous habits are _____ and _____.

CHAPTER NINE

Joe

1. What type of car does Joe like to drive?
2. What does Joe do when no one is looking?
3. What does Joe's dad do for a living?
4. In what town did Joe grow up?
5. Who was Joe named after?

Multiple choice

6. Joe's eyes are:
   a) blue, b) brown, c) hazel, d) green
7. Growing up, Joe liked to play:
   a) baseball, b) hockey, c) tennis, d) football
8. Joe began to sing on stage at the age of:
   a) 3,   b) 10,   c) 5,   d) 13

NEW KIDS TRIVIA BOOK

9. Joe's newest sporting love is:
   a) running, b) golf, c) tennis, d) ice skating
10. Joe has a pet dog named:
    a) Misty, b) Buster, c) Boe, d) Alex

True or False

11. Joe prefers to hang out in comfortable clothes.
12. Joe never daydreams.
13. Joe does impressions of the other New Kids.
14. Joe hates to cook.
15. Joe hates to lose at anything.

NEW KIDS TRIVIA BOOK

Fill in the Blanks

16. Joe served as an _____ in his church.
17. As a youngster Joe starred in the shows _____ and _____.
18. Joe went to _____ parochial school.
19. Joe joined New Kids before his _____ birthday.
20. Joe likes reading a good _____ novel.

CHAPTER TEN

Discography & Videography

New Kids Albums

NEW KIDS ON THE BLOCK
(Columbia, 1986; rereleased 1989)

Songs:

"Stop It Girl"
"Didn't I (Blow Your Mind)"
"Angel"
"Popsicle"
"Be My Girl"
"New Kids on the Block"
"Are You Down?"
"I Wanna Be Loved By You"
"Don't Give Up On Me"
"Treat Me Right"

HANGIN' TOUGH
(Columbia, 1988)

Songs:
"You Got It (The Right Stuff)"
"Please Don't Go Girl"
"I'll Be Loving You (Forever)"
"Cover Girl"
"I Need You"
"Hangin' Tough"
"I Remember When"
"Wha'Cha Gonna Do (About It)"
"My Favorite Girl"
"Hold On"

MERRY, MERRY CHRISTMAS
(Columbia, 1989)

Songs:
"This One's For the Children"
"Last Night I Saw Santa Claus"
"I'll Be Missin' You Come Christmas (A Letter to Santa)"
"I Still Believe in Santa Claus"
"Merry, Merry Christmas"
"The Christmas Song (Chestnuts Roasting on an Open Fire)"
"Funky, Funky Xmas"
"White Christmas"
"Little Drummer Boy"

NEW KIDS TRIVIA BOOK

New Kids Singles

"Be My Girl"
"Stop It Girl"
"Didn't I (Blow Your Mind)"
"Please Don't Go Girl"
"You Got It (The Right Stuff)"
"Hangin' Tough"
"Cover Girl"
"This One's For the Children"

New Kids Music Videos

Please Don't Go Girl
You Got It (The Right Stuff)
I'll Be Loving You (Forever)
Hangin' Tough
Didn't I (Blow Your Mind)
Cover Girl
This One's For the Children

NEW KIDS TRIVIA BOOK

New Kids Video Cassettes

NEW KIDS ON THE BLOCK–HANGIN' TOUGH
(CBS Home Video, 1989)

Songs:

"Please Don't Go Girl"
"You Got It (The Right Stuff)"
"I'll Be Loving You (Forever)"
"Hangin' Tough"

NEW KIDS ON THE BLOCK– HANGIN' TOUGH LIVE
(CBS Home Video, 1989)

Songs:

"My Favorite Girl"
"What'Cha Gonna Do (About It)"
"Please Don't Go Girl"
"Cover Girl"
"You Got It (The Right Stuff)"
"I'll Be Loving You (Forever)"
"Hangin' Tough"

Answers

CHAPTER ONE

1. Joe
2. Donnie
3. Jon
4. Jordan
5. Danny
6. Jordan
7. Jon
8. Joe
9. Donnie
10. Danny

11. c
12. a
13. b
14. c
15. d
16. a
17. d
18. b
19. c
20. a

21. True
22. False
23. True
24. True
25. False
26. False
27. True
28. False
29. True
30. True

31. Jon and Jordan
32. Misty and Buster
33. Danny
34. Michael Jackson
35. Joe
36. fruit
37. dark brown, brown
38. Puff McCloud, Woody Woodpecker
39. bowling
40. Saab 900 convertible
41. c
42. a
43. d
44. e
45. b

NEW KIDS TRIVIA BOOK

46. PLEASE DON'T GO GIRL
47. TREAT ME RIGHT
48. COVER GIRL
49. ARE YOU DOWN?
50. THIS ONE'S FOR THE CHILDREN

CHAPTER TWO

1. Maurice Starr
2. New Edition
3. Bobby Brown
4. Mary Alford
5. 1984
6. July 4th Statue of Liberty festival
7. "Let's Dance" by David Bowie
8. A Big Wheel
9. Columbia
10. 1986
11. d
12. a
13. b
14. c
15. a
16. d
17. b
18. c
19. a
20. b
21. False
22. False
23. True
24. True
25. True
26. False
27. False
28. True
29. False
30. True
31. Danny, Donnie, Jon, and Jordan
32. William Monroe Trotter
33. Alma and Donald, Sr.
34. Marlene and Allan
35. Kay and Thomas
36. Elizabeth and Daniel, Sr.

NEW KIDS TRIVIA BOOK

37. Eight
38. Five
39. Four
40. Eight
41. d
42. a
43. e
44. c
45. b

New Kids Secret Code Answer

DON'T YOU JUST LOVE DONNIE'S JEANS

CHAPTER THREE

1. *New Kids on the Block*
2. *Hangin' Tough*
3. "Be My Girl"
4. *Merry, Merry Christmas*
5. "This One's for the Children"
6. "Some Things Never Change"
7. "Please Don't Go Girl"
8. Rhythm & Blues
9. Huey Lewis and the News
10. "You Make Me Feel Brand New"
11. b
12. a
13. d
14. a
15. c
16. b
17. d
18. c
19. a
20. b
21. True
22. False
23. True
24. False
25. False
26. True
27. False
28. True

NEW KIDS TRIVIA BOOK

29. False
30. True
31. Tina Turner, George Michael
32. Apollo
33. The Osmonds
34. The five hardest working kids in show business
35. United Cerebral Palsy
36. bike-a-thon
37. New Kids on the Block
38. their work in the fight against drug abuse
39. "You Got It (The Right Stuff)"
40. Producer of the Year
41. b
42. c
43. a

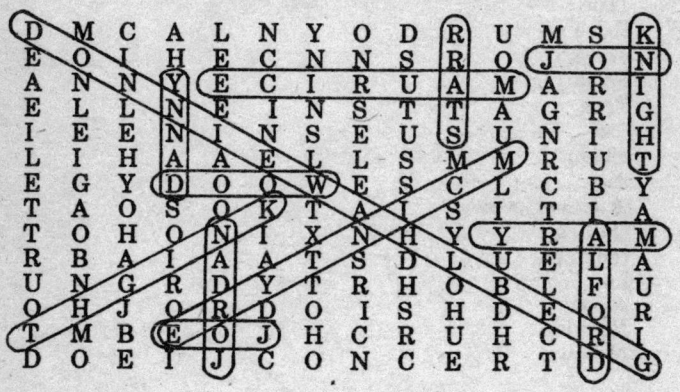

NEW KIDS WORD SEARCH ANSWER

CHAPTER FOUR

1. Danny
2. Jordan
3. Donnie
4. Joe
5. Jon
6. Donnie
7. Joe
8. Danny
9. Jon
10. Jordan

NEW KIDS TRIVIA BOOK

11. e
12. c
13. b
14. a
15. d
16. a
17. b
18. e
19. c
20. d
21. False
22. False
23. True
24. True
25. False
26. True
27. False
28. False
29. False
30. True
31. bad
32. video
33. rap
34. practical jokes
35. clothes
36. cooking
37. hotel room
38. school
39. Renaldo
40. Motown

CHAPTER FIVE

1. Teddy
2. He drove a food delivery truck
3. The Boston Red Sox
4. Dorchester
5. Roxbury
6. c
7. b
8. d
9. a
10. b

62

NEW KIDS TRIVIA BOOK

11. True
12. False
13. True
14. True
15. False
16. Oreos
17. black, gold
18. Seiko Matsuda
19. The Northside Boys
20. One Nation

CHAPTER SIX

1. his mother's father
2. a teddy bear puppet
3. he was a U.S. Post Office mail carrier
4. Disney World
5. Donnie
6. c
7. b
8. a
9. d
10. a
11. True
12. False
13. False
14. True
15. True
16. black, brown
17. Cher
18. Jeep Cherokee
19. Christmas
20. "I'm outta here!"

CHAPTER SEVEN

1. to visit his grandparents in Canada
2. carpentry and gardening
3. The Stylistics
4. *This Old House*
5. 4 U MA!

NEW KIDS TRIVIA BOOK

6.	c	11.	True	16.	Thayer Academy
7.	a	12.	False	17.	Donnie
8.	c	13.	True	18.	Mickey Mouse
9.	d	14.	False	19.	ski, swim
10.	b	15.	True	20.	5,000

CHAPTER EIGHT

1. Julius Cæsar
2. guitar
3. Danny
4. by listening to music on his stereo
5. yes, and it drives Jon crazy!

6. d	11.	False
7. a	12.	True
8. c	13.	False
9. b	14.	True
10. d	15.	False

16. Catholic Memorial
17. supernatural things
18. *Batman*
19. Tommy Page
20. biting his nails, twirling his hair

CHAPTER NINE

1. convertibles
2. he makes funny faces
3. he's a bricklayer
4. Needham, Mass.
5. St. Joseph

6. a
7. d
8. c
9. b
10. c

11. True
12. False
13. True
14. False
15. True

16. altar boy
17. *Oliver, The Music Man*
18. St. Mary's
19. 13th
20. mystery